Tokyo Heat

NIGHTS SERIES BOOK THREE

A.M. SALINGER

COPYRIGHT

Tokyo Heat (Nights Series Book 3)
Copyright © 2018 by A.M. Salinger
All rights reserved.
Registered with the US Copyright Office.
Second paperback edition: 2024
ISBN: 978-1-9996184-2-1

www.AMSalinger.com
shop.adstarrling.com

Edited by www.ElfwerksEditing.com
Cover Design by A.M. Salinger

Miles - 7

Urban Fantasy Romance written as

Ava Marie Salinger

Fallen Messengers

Fractured Souls - 1

Spellbound - 2

Edge Lines - 3

Oathbreaker - 4

Harbinger - 5

Crimson Skies - 6

Wicked - Fallen Messengers Short Story Collection

CHAPTER ONE

Shit!

Gabe gave his inbox a final glance, logged off, and rose from his desk. He glanced out of the panoramic windows to his left as he shrugged into his suit jacket.

Dusk cast red and orange streaks across the sky above Tokyo, the light washing through the glass and painting amber shadows on the crisp white walls of his office. He looked at his watch, cursed under his breath, and grabbed his bag.

He was five minutes late.

Gabe's gaze collided with a curious stare as he turned toward the door. A man with dark blond hair and blue eyes stood watching him, one shoulder propped against the frame.

"Got plans for the weekend?" he drawled, cocking an elegant eyebrow.

Gabe smiled, hoping his restlessness didn't show.

"Yes, I do."

Rhys Damon studied him for a moment longer before letting out a sigh.

"Ah, to be in love and shacked up."

Gabe felt his ears grow warm at his boss's teasing expression.

"I wouldn't go as far as that," he mumbled.

"I thought you'd moved in with him," Rhys said, surprise flashing in his blue gaze. "What's it been? Six months?"

"I did, and it's been six and a half," Gabe muttered. *Not that I'm counting.*

He swallowed a groan at Rhys's sudden sly grin.

"I just sent you the final plans for the Hudson resort," Gabe said. "Let me know—"

"*Rhys!*" someone suddenly barked from across the expanse of the open-plan office space outside.

They turned and stared at the hulking, dark-haired man standing in the doorway of a glass room on the opposite side of the floor. Wade Tucker—the other brain behind the incredibly successful, multi-award-winning Chicago-based design firm currently taking Tokyo by storm—scowled at Rhys.

Rhys grimaced.

"It seems the big bad wolf has awakened." He glanced at Gabe. "Quick, run before he sinks his teeth into you too."

Gabe hurried toward the elevator and glanced over his shoulder at the two men facing each other stiffly across the empty office. He doubted he was the only one who had noticed the increasing tension between the firm's partners over the last year.

Best friends since their college days, Rhys Damon and Wade Tucker had followed in each other's footsteps throughout their early careers, often as rivals bidding for the same contracts. They'd finally set up shop as Damon & Tucker. Twelve years on and their company was now among the top twenty in the business for luxury interior design, consulting, and branding, catering to some of the most exclusive resorts and hotel chains around the world, as well as affluent private clients.

All thoughts of his bosses' woes fled Gabe's mind when he exited the lift and entered the lobby of the glass-and-steel edifice that housed the Tokyo branch of the firm.

A man stood leaning against a navy-blue Jaguar saloon parked at the curb outside, hands tucked in the pockets of his tailored suit and powerful legs crossed at the ankles. He seemed oblivious to the stares he was drawing from the passersby and office workers leaving the building, his eyes focused on the foyer.

Although the car was a stunning piece of art and engineering, Gabe knew it was its dark-haired owner who had captured the avid interest of the men and women openly ogling him.

Gabe's pulse jumped when he met the man's gunmetal stare through the glass wall. He still couldn't quite believe that he was going out with Cam Sorvino, the king of one-night stands. His gaze dropped from Cam's stunning face and full lips, to his stubbled jaw and hard physique.

Nor can I believe I've had sex with that gorgeous body.

Heat warmed Gabe's cheeks when he recalled the last time they'd shared a bed.

It had been over a week ago, a fact that had obviously frustrated Cam as he barely let Gabe sleep that night. His job as an asset manager for one of the biggest investment firms in Asia had taken him to Singapore for most of the last month and he only returned to Tokyo on the weekends, often late on Saturday afternoons.

Though Gabe loved nothing more than being in Cam's arms, he knew the commute was taking its toll on his lover, which was why he'd asked Cam to fly back early this week.

Cam's gaze grew heavy-lidded as Gabe crossed the sidewalk and approached the car. Gabe knew that if it wasn't for the people around them, Cam would have pulled him into his embrace and kissed him senseless. Gabe stifled a sigh, somewhat grateful for their audience.

Once they started touching each other, there would be no stopping them. And Cam's libido had turned voracious as of late, his appetite not even remotely quenched until they'd had at least four rounds of toe-curling sex and Gabe's voice was hoarse from crying and moaning in pleasure.

"I've packed us a couple of overnight bags, like you instructed," Cam said in a smoky voice that sent tingles down Gabe's spine as he opened the passenger door of the Jag. "So, where are we headed, Mr. Anderson?"

Gabe slipped onto the cream leather seat and

waited until Cam climbed in beside him before giving him the address of the place he'd booked them in for the weekend.

Cam raised an eyebrow.

"The beach?" His lips curved. "Does this mean I get to see you in swim trunks?"

Gabe's pulse skittered at the passionate gleam in the gray eyes watching him.

"It's a hot springs, so, no."

Cam grinned.

"Even better. You'll be naked."

Gabe rolled his eyes as Cam started the engine and steered the Jag around.

Although the drive to the Izu Peninsula took over two hours, the time flew by while they chatted about their week, soft jazz music playing from the speakers as the vehicle ate away the miles.

Cam's eyes widened when he drove into the paved courtyard of the traditional Japanese inn sitting on the small spur of land jutting out from the coastline, the headlights briefly illuminating the golden stretch of sand leading to the Pacific Ocean. He parked the car, his gaze lingering on the open vista before switching to Gabe.

"Nice."

Gabe smiled, a flutter of excitement sending his pulse racing at the night he'd planned for them.

"I'm glad you like it."

They collected their bags from the trunk and headed for the entrance.

Cam hesitated when they reached the porch, his hand on the handle of the front door.

"You didn't design this one too, did you?"

Gabe blinked. His ears grew hot as he suddenly recollected the exclusive Tokyo hotel where they'd first made love a year ago. It was where he'd also rather splendidly lost his cherry to the magnificent man beside him. Gabe's cock twitched as he thought of that night. Though sex with Cam always blew his mind, their first time together was incredibly precious to Gabe.

It was Cam who had finally helped him overcome the trauma of his past, when he'd nearly been raped by five men who'd paid his then boyfriend to tape their vile acts on camera, leaving him unable to sleep with anyone for over eight years despite regularly seeing a therapist. The gentle yet passionate way Cam had made love to him that time, how Cam had engraved his touch and scent on Gabe's body until he utterly and completely lost himself in the act, how he'd brought Gabe to one earth-shattering climax after another—all of it were priceless memories Gabe would take to his grave. Not that he would ever admit this to Cam.

Gabe chuckled at his lover's guarded expression.

"No, I didn't design this place."

Relief flashed across Cam's face.

"Good. I'd seriously feel as if I were committing blasphemy otherwise." Cam sniffed. "Not that sex with you isn't the most unholy, wicked thing I've ever experienced in my life. I mean, there's some stuff we've done that I—"

"Shut up, Cam!" Gabe hissed, clamping a hand over Cam's mouth as a hostess headed across the foyer toward them.

Cam grinned and licked Gabe's palm. Gabe swallowed a groan at the tingle that shot through him.

This erotic asshole.

CHAPTER TWO

Appreciation dawned in Cam's eyes as they were led through the luxurious ryokan to their private suite. The five-star inn only housed fifteen rooms, which made it that much more intimate for the guests willing to pay the high three-figure-a-night fee it cost to stay there.

Cam paused inside their room and scanned the beautiful blend of traditional and modern furniture occupying the open-plan living space while Gabe thanked their hostess before she left the room. On the opposite side of an expanse of dark wood floor, next to a king-size bed set on a raised platform, sliding doors led to a terrace and a large, private open-air bath overlooking the beachfront and the ocean beyond. Lanterns cast a mellow light on the steam rising from the still surface of the spring waters, the distant sound of the surf crashing on the shoreline a rhythmic lullaby.

Cam soundlessly crossed the floor and trailed his

hand along the bottle of champagne sitting in an ice bucket on a low table by the sliding doors. He smiled at Gabe and slowly licked the drops of condensation on his fingertips.

Gabe shivered, anticipation coiling at the base of his spine at the teasing light in Cam's eyes and the sight of Cam's pink tongue dragging across his skin.

"Really nice," Cam murmured. He popped the cork and poured the foaming, golden liquid into the two champagne glasses on the tray before handing one to Gabe. "So, when do I get to eat you?"

Gabe's jaw fell open. He groaned when he registered Cam's keen expression.

"You fucking sex demon. The only thing you're gonna be eating in the next hour is dinner, so behave yourself."

Cam pursed his lips, fake disappointment twisting his handsome features.

"That's too bad."

A hot gleam darkened Cam's eyes when he spied what lay on the bed. It was a pair of yukatas, the traditional kimonos favored at Japanese inns.

"I wonder if they'll indulge my request to serve dinner on your naked body," Cam muttered absentmindedly.

Gabe nearly choked on his champagne. The torrid image that flashed across his mind, of Cam's strong white teeth nibbling him from his head all the way to his toes, had his cock throbbing.

"No way!" Gabe said, flushing.

Cam waggled his eyebrows. "I got you thinking about it though, didn't I?"

Gabe chuckled at his lover's playful expression. "You horny bastard."

❧

CAM GLANCED AT GABE WHERE HE WASHED HIMSELF under the outdoor shower next to him. They'd finished dinner a while back and had spent the last hour sitting on the terrace, talking and drinking sake while they enjoyed the balmy night air, Japan's summer heat moderated by the cool breeze blowing off the ocean.

The sexual tension that wound around and between them as the minutes ticked by had sent a shiver of excitement running through Cam. They had changed into the yukatas for their meal. The way the silvery garment hugged Gabe's body and allowed Cam tantalizing glimpses of his lover's chest and thighs made him decide there and then to buy him several of the damn things just so he could peel them off him when they had sex.

"Want to get in the bath?" Gabe had finally murmured, color high on his cheekbones.

Cam had smiled at his sweetly shy expression. Even though they'd made love hundreds of times before, Gabe's adorable bashfulness on occasions like this never failed to bring out Cam's possessive nature. The fact that the bewitchingly gorgeous man sitting opposite him belonged to him, body and soul, was something Cam truly relished.

He'd nodded his acquiescence and watched as Gabe disrobed and walked to the first outdoor shower. Gabe's broad shoulders as the water flowed on him, the transparent streams racing down the delicious curve of his spine and over his gorgeous butt before dripping into the shadowy space at the apex of his strong thighs and running down his legs—all of it had Cam's mouth watering in anticipation. He'd shrugged off his own kimono and joined Gabe under the second shower, anxious to start their foreplay.

Cam could tell Gabe was conscious of his penetrating gaze from the way his ears flamed and his dick swelled up against his toned belly, just as he himself was conscious of Gabe's fleeting glances. He turned off the shower a moment later and ran his fingers through his hair, pretending to ignore Gabe's eyes on him as he stood gloriously naked next to him, his own cock at full mast.

Four steps took Cam to the open-air bath. He slipped into the hot water, glanced at the box of condoms and the bottle of lube within hand's reach, and turned to watch Gabe as he turned off the shower.

Cam's cock throbbed at the sight of a flushed and clearly aroused Gabe staring hotly at him.

"Come here," he murmured.

CHAPTER THREE

GABE COMPLIED AND SLID INTO THE BATH NEXT TO CAM. Cam reached out and pulled Gabe into his arms, ripples sloshing around them. They both groaned when their bodies touched, chest-to-chest and groin-to-groin, Gabe's hard shaft rising out of the water to rub against Cam's straining dick.

Cam cradled Gabe's face in his hands and kissed him hungrily, like a starving man feasting on his last meal. Gabe opened his lips and allowed Cam inside, his own tongue rising eagerly to meet Cam's.

Heat shot to Gabe's cock at the electrifying way Cam was claiming his mouth. He moaned and melted against Cam, hands rising to grip his lover's shoulders, fingers biting into the taut flesh as pleasure pulsed through him.

Cam dropped his hands to Gabe's back and ran them down his spine, fingers massaging the tense muscles under his fingertips. Cam dipped his hands in the water and squeezed the firm, toned flesh of Gabe's butt. Gabe arched, his hips flexing reflexively against Cam's. Cam swallowed Gabe's throaty gasp and slid a finger down Gabe's cleft until he found his tight opening.

Gabe stiffened when Cam played with the puckered folds, anticipation sending a delicious spasm deep inside his passage. He spread his legs to allow Cam better access and reached down to palm their hard cocks, his fingers rubbing the both of them while Cam continued teasing him beneath the surface of the water.

Cam growled and moved his lips to Gabe's left ear, nipping at the lobe. Gabe shuddered, his hole squeezing tight before slowly opening.

"*Oh!*" Gabe's ears flamed as the hot water seeped inside his body.

Cam slipped the tip of his index finger inside Gabe and slowly ran it around the tight rim of his hole.

Gabe cursed and twitched as fiery tingles sparked through his entire body from where Cam played with his entrance. He accelerated his strokes on their cocks, his breath coming in hard pants as his fingers worked their wet shafts. Cam groaned and bit Gabe's neck gently before suddenly grabbing him by the waist. He lifted him up and plopped him down on the edge of the bath.

Gabe gasped when Cam parted his knees and lifted his legs up in the air, driving him back onto his elbows. Cam hooked Gabe's calves over his shoulders, pushed his thighs back toward his chest, and dipped his head to swallow Gabe's aching cock.

Gabe cried out, head falling back while he rolled his hips, his ass lifting off the wooden deck as pleasure rippled through him. Gabe moaned as Cam worked his stiff cock with his lips and tongue, repeatedly teasing the sensitive head with flicks and whirls before nibbling and sucking the glistening, veiny shaft and Gabe's tightening balls.

Gabe dug his heels into Cam's back as his orgasm raced through him, hips pumping erratically as he fucked Cam's hot mouth, blood roaring in his ears while his cries echoed around the terrace. He reached down and fisted his fingers in Cam's hair just as his cock pulsed violently, his breath locking in his throat as the insane pleasure of the earth-shattering climax Cam had brought him to washed over him. Cam grunted and swallowed Gabe's cum as if it was the finest elixir, his jaw and tongue working deeply as they milked his shaft to the very end.

Gabe shuddered and groaned when Cam finally pulled his lips from his trembling cock. Cam rose above him and palmed his own dick, his hand establishing a fast rhythm as he stroked his engorged flesh toward an orgasm.

Gabe sat up and moved Cam's fingers aside. He gripped Cam's hips, bowed his head, and took Cam in his mouth, eager to taste his man.

CAM HISSED, FIRE LICKING THROUGH HIS ENTIRE BODY from where Gabe's lips and tongue sucked and played with his throbbing shaft. Cam twisted his hands in Gabe's hair and held him in place while he thrust in and out of his delicious mouth, balls clenching at his impending orgasm, his senses still drowning in the intoxicating scent of Gabe's recent climax.

Cam grunted and exploded on Gabe's tongue a moment later, pleasure tightening his spine and legs, his hips rolling wildly as he sprayed his cum down the back of Gabe's hot throat.

Cam withdrew his hard cock from Gabe's greedy lips, ripped a condom open, and sheathed himself under his lover's heated gaze. Gabe poured lube in one hand and reached down to finger himself, his face flushed with desire. Cam paused, the sight before his eyes so electrifying he could only stop and stare.

Sweet Jesus.

Gabe was lying on his back with his feet flat on the edge of the deck and his thighs spread wide. His cock swelled with fresh arousal as he dipped two fingers in and out of his hole, stretching his entrance for Cam, his eyes cobalt with passion and his mouth open on labored pants.

Cam groaned, lubed his sheathed dick, and coated his hand liberally with the slippery liquid before pressing it to Gabe's opening. Gabe lay back and sexily tugged his lower lip between his teeth as Cam took over readying him, two fingers gliding slickly in and out of his heated passage.

"Cam!" Gabe moaned breathlessly. He flexed his hips as Cam thrust a third finger inside him. "Please, I want it—*now!*"

Fuck.

Cam scissored his fingers in Gabe's hole a couple of times before slipping out of his body. He grabbed Gabe's ass and tugged him closer, positioning Gabe's opening flush against his sheathed dick where he stood at the edge of the bath.

Gabe wrapped his legs around Cam's waist and reached up to grab Cam's shoulders, the hungry sounds he was making sending a trail of fire shooting to Cam's groin.

Cam impaled Gabe in one thrust, his aching cock gliding inside Gabe's smooth passage to the hilt. Cam fixed Gabe's ass into position and flexed and rolled his hips, repeatedly plunging his hard shaft into him, setting a punishing pace that had Gabe going wild beneath him and sent the bath water roiling noisily around Cam's thighs.

They climaxed a moment later, the ecstasy of their coupling too great for either of them to bear. Cam slipped out of Gabe's body, discarded the first condom, and pulled a second one over his still-erect cock, sweat dripping down his face and his muscles trembling with tension. He entered Gabe while the latter's passage still shivered and throbbed from his orgasm and leaned down over him, hands braced on either side of Gabe's head.

Gabe groaned and bit down on Cam's shoulder as they started their fierce mating once more, his heels digging into Cam's ass while his nails raked his back, his hungry hole pulsing and spasming around Cam's dick.

Cam lost himself in the man beneath him, taking him, fucking him like he'd been dying to do for over a week. He drove them both over the edge again and again, their guttural grunts of ecstasy filling the suite, Gabe's chest and belly growing slick and sticky with sweat and cum from his multiple orgasms.

It wasn't until they'd both climaxed repeatedly that Cam finally slowed, his legs weak where he stood in the bath, his aching dick still wedged deep inside Gabe's shivering passage. He slipped out, peeled the condom off, and covered Gabe with his body where he lay on his back on the deck.

Gabe shuddered and twitched beneath him, his arms coming up to wrap around Cam's shoulders while his legs stayed firmly locked around his waist.

"Love you," Gabe whispered in Cam's right ear, his heated pants still labored and his voice dazed with pleasure. "I love you, Cam."

Cam stilled, his breath freezing in his throat at the murmured confession. He ignored the sudden icy band gripping his heart, rose up onto his elbows, and kissed Gabe fiercely.

CHAPTER FOUR

GABE CLOSED THE DOOR AND STARED AT THE DARK apartment. Two weeks had passed since their trip to the hot springs. Cam hadn't come home once since that weekend, his job keeping him working all the hours that God made in Singapore as his team raced to close a major deal. Gabe suspected that Cam was probably thankful for the distraction. Although they'd spent the rest of that weekend at the inn making love, Gabe knew the words he had spoken that first night had created a distance between them. Gabe had seen it deep in the gunmetal eyes watching him whenever Cam thought he wasn't looking, a pensive, preoccupied look that spoke of a man wrestling with his inner demons.

Gabe sighed, dropped his bag on an armchair, and headed into the state-of-the-art kitchen. He grabbed a beer from the fridge and popped the cap before taking a swig of the amber liquid, his mind brimming with the thousand and one thoughts that had filled his every waking moment for the past weeks.

Gabe knew that Cam loved him. Cam expressed it every time they kissed, every time they touched, every time he thrust his powerful body into Gabe's. Gabe was also conscious of the fact that Cam would probably never tell him the three words he most wanted to hear.

Although Gabe was grateful for their current relationship, his growing hunger for Cam meant he wanted his everything. His body, his mind, his soul. And his heart.

Gabe wanted those three little words.

Craved them like a thirsty man longing for a single drop of water.

But Cam was not a man who could easily give himself to anyone. Not while the scars of his past remained so fresh.

It was in the third month of their relationship that Cam had finally opened up to Gabe about his childhood. As Gabe cradled Cam's head to his chest where they lay together in bed and listened to his horrific confessions, his heart had broken for the ten-year-old boy who had walked in on his mother while she was in her final death throes from a drug overdose. Though Gabe's own relationship with his parents had become strained after he came out of the closet while he was in college, at least they were still alive.

Cam had spoken of his harrowing time in the various institutions where he'd spent his early teens until he met Joe Cavendish, his best friend and the owner of *Saron,* the club where Gabe and Cam had met. Despite the emotion choking his throat, Gabe had chuckled at the two teenagers' various escapades as they had grown up, always there for one another and watching each other's backs.

Gabe's fingers had clenched in Cam's hair when he told him of the night he and Joe had finally run away from the children's home at age fifteen. It had been a stupid, brave, inane, and life-changing act—one that had sent their futures spiraling in vastly different directions and landed them in careers they could never have anticipated in a million years.

Though they'd tried to keep in touch, fate had torn the two friends apart and they'd spent the next few years treading different paths in the same city, neither realizing they were living just a few miles from the other. While Cam had worked all hours in several manual jobs and often went without food while he studied for his SATs in public libraries, Joe had been lured into the sex and strip club scene, his tall, alluring physique making him out to be older than he looked.

That they had found each other again twenty years later, in a country on the other side of the world, was a miracle both men had welcomed. Yet, despite their rekindled friendship and the fact that they were both wealthy and successful beyond their wildest dreams, the pair had struggled to let go of the darkness that still clouded their hearts.

It had taken nearly losing the man he loved at the hands of a vicious stalker for Joe Cavendish to finally overcome his demons and admit his feelings for Ethan Skye, one of the bartenders at *Saron* and Gabe's closest friend in the city. That Ethan had harbored shocking secrets of his own had stunned all of them when they were accidentally revealed by a mutual friend nearly a year ago. Ethan's deliberate, yet justifiable deception, would have jeopardized the two men's burgeoning relationship had Joe not utterly and completely fallen for Ethan. The way they now openly loved and teased one another sometimes sent a pang of envy through Gabe.

He flicked on the lights as he walked through the apartment, his gaze sweeping the empty space. Though more than half a year had passed since he moved into Cam's place and made it his home, Gabe could still see and feel his lover everywhere he looked—from the sleek lines of expensive furniture and the masculine decor, to Cam's belongings scattered here and there.

Gabe showered, ate dinner, and went to bed. His cell had remained silent that day, Cam evidently too busy to respond to the text Gabe had sent at lunchtime. Gabe placed the phone on the nightstand and pulled the covers back. Heat flooded his cheeks when he saw the shirt lying on the sheets.

It was one of Cam's.

Gabe climbed in the bed and settled on his back before reaching for the garment. He blushed and buried his face in it, inhaling the scent of the man he loved.

Like all the nights since he'd last seen Cam, Gabe reached down and touched his aching cock, one hand wrapping around his hardening shaft and setting a slow, punishing rhythm while he imagined Cam touching him.

A moan left Gabe's throat as he dipped his hand

lower and touched his hole, his index finger slick with his pre-cum. He bit his lip and squeezed tightly, like Cam had taught him, before opening himself to his touch. He ran the pad of his finger around his sensitive rim and plunged deep inside, a second finger quickly joining the first one.

Tension wound through Gabe as he rubbed his cock and finger-fucked himself, his ass lifting off the pillow as he bowed his back. His orgasm came too fast, his hips flexing up toward the ceiling, his ass clenching around his fingers while he pumped cum out into his hand, his labored grunts echoing around the room. Though his climax had his toes curling in the sheets, it wasn't enough.

Gabe closed his eyes and shuddered, an ache building deep inside him. Only Cam could give him the pleasure his body craved and the gratification his heart and soul sought.

CAM DROPPED INTO THE HOTEL CHAIR AND CLOSED HIS eyes. It was past midnight in Singapore and he'd just finished at the office. He fished his cell out of his pocket and hesitated as he stared at Gabe's message.

The words Gabe had spoken in the aftermath of their lovemaking a fortnight ago at the hot springs still haunted Cam. His confession had sent a chill through Cam's bones that had only grown in the time they'd been apart, a thorn that twisted and stabbed at his cold heart.

Even though he cared deeply for Gabe, Cam didn't think he could give him what he wanted. A fully loving, committed relationship. And Gabe deserved that more than anyone Cam knew—deserved to be happy, deserved to be cherished like the precious gift that he was.

Deep down inside, Cam knew there might be a time when he would be forced to let Gabe go. Cam didn't know if he would be selfless enough to do that though, when that time came. Didn't think he could easily give Gabe to another man. Didn't think he could relinquish the possessive feelings he harbored for him despite the fact that he couldn't return Gabe's love.

Cam groaned and dropped his face in his hands. He wanted nothing more right now than to forget the storm of conflicting emotions raging through his heart and mind. And he knew of only one way to do this.

He wanted to see Gabe. To kiss him. To touch him. To take him. To watch him come beneath him, body impaled by Cam's cock, hole clenching and sucking Cam deeper into his body, fingers and heels digging into Cam's flesh while he arched and cried out in pleasure.

Cam felt his dick stiffen behind his zipper. He stumbled to the shower, stripped, and jerked off twice under the steaming water, the image of Gabe's climaxing face imprinted on his inner vision as he stroked himself to his own shuddering orgasms.

CHAPTER FIVE

Gabe startled when his cell rang. He finished knotting his tie and strode to the nightstand. Relief flashed through him when he saw the caller ID. He picked up the phone and touched the screen.

"Hey," Cam said across the connection. The sound of traffic and a busy street rose in the background.

"Hey," Gabe murmured. He glanced at his watch. "Aren't you supposed to be at the office already?"

"I'm walking to the building right now. We had a late night at work, so I told the team to come in an hour after normal starting time."

Jealousy stabbed through Gabe at Cam's words. Although he knew Cam would not cheat on him, the fact that he was spending all his time with men and women who probably wanted to sleep with him made Gabe oddly resentful.

"That's great," Gabe said, trying not to grit his teeth. "When do you think you'll be home?"

Gabe winced at the way his words had come out.

Jesus, I sound like his wife.

There was a pause at the other end of the line.

"Probably not this weekend either. We're snowed under trying to seal this deal."

Pain lanced through Gabe's chest at Cam's carefully neutral voice. He took a shaky breath, wondering if his lover missed him as much as he did.

"Okay," Gabe managed. "I'll be out late tonight, so don't worry if I don't answer my phone."

"Oh." Surprise tinged Cam's voice. "You going out with your colleagues?"

Gabe ran a hand through his hair and stared blindly through the glass wall of their bedroom at the sunlit city beyond the terrace that ran the length of their apartment.

"No, I'll be at *Saron.*"

Silence descended on the line.

"You've been going there a lot lately," Cam finally said.

Gabe stilled and blinked. "Yeah, so?" he murmured, puzzled by Cam's strangely bitter undertone.

A sigh sounded on the line.

"So, I don't like it when you go there without me," Cam said with frustrated possessiveness.

Gabe's eyes widened. He stared at his cell for a moment, not quite believing his ears. A bolt of irritation stabbed through him.

This self-centered prick.

Gabe kept his voice cool as he responded to Cam. "And why is that? Joe and Ethan are our friends, so I don't quite see what you're objecting to—"

"I don't like the way the men there look at you, okay?" Cam snapped. "Those guys always strip you with their eyes, even when I'm standing right next to you!"

Gabe nearly dropped the cell in shock. He gaped at the screen, his heart thundering in his chest.

"Gabe, you still there?" Cam barked.

"Yeah," Gabe mumbled, uncertain of how to react to Cam's blatant jealousy.

"Don't go to *Saron*," Cam ordered.

Gabe opened and closed his mouth soundlessly at Cam's haughty command. Fury surged through him in the next instant.

What an asshole!

"That is the most asinine thing you've ever said to me, Cam Sorvino!" Gabe hissed. "Now, reflect on your goddamn words and apologize to me when you've come to your fucking senses!"

Gabe ended the call and dropped the phone on the bed, his hands shaking.

The cell rang five seconds later. Gabe hesitated before picking it up.

"Yes?"

"I forbid you to go there!" Cam growled.

Gabe scowled. "Oh, yeah? Well, try and stop me, you narcissistic moron!"

Gabe disconnected and turned the phone off when it started blaring again.

"Wow," Ethan Skye murmured. "What a giant dick."

Gabe grimaced as he gazed at the blond bartender.

"I know, right?"

Ethan finished mixing a drink and served it to the man who'd ordered it. He hesitated as he turned to Gabe where the latter sat on a barstool at *Saron's* counter, chin resting in his hand while he gloomily nursed his Scotch.

"I kinda know what he means though," Ethan said. "Not that I'm saying he's right," he added at Gabe's frown. "It's just—well, there's no other way to say this." He took a deep breath. "You're—"

"An incredible hottie that any man would die to have under him and any woman would kill to have above her," muttered the handsome guy with black-rimmed specs beside Ethan.

Gabe gaped at Akihito, one of the other bartenders.

Ethan shrugged. "Yup, that pretty much sums it up."

Akihito waved a finger under Gabe's stunned face. "And I'm saying this as a happily married man with a kid." He moved to the other end of the bar and started serving customers.

Gabe groaned and placed his hands over his hot face.

"Maybe you need to teach Cam a lesson," Ethan said pensively. He narrowed his green eyes at Gabe. "Hey, you tried topping him?"

Gabe's elbows slipped from the counter as he nearly fell off the barstool.

"*No!*"

Gabe's ears flamed as he imagined himself taking

Cam. He shook his head vehemently, the mental picture anathema to him.

"Nuh-uh!" he repeated doggedly.

Ethan arched an eyebrow.

"Really? I've thought about topping Joe."

A hand landed on Ethan's head and briskly ruffled his hair.

"What bullshit are you spouting now?" Joe Cavendish said as he loomed over the bartender.

Ethan brightened and gazed eagerly at his lover.

"I was talking about topping you."

Joe blinked lazily at Ethan, his unfazed expression eliciting a surge of admiration from Gabe.

"Not happening," he said gruffly.

Joe turned toward the shelves and grabbed a bottle of Scotch.

"How about I finger you?" Ethan suggested.

Oh God. Gabe considered putting his hands over his ears.

"Nope," Joe muttered, pouring himself a double serving.

"Lick you?" Ethan proposed.

Gabe groaned. *Sweet Jesus.*

Joe dropped ice into his tumbler and narrowed his eyes at Ethan.

"No."

Ethan pursed his lips. "How about if I just *look* at it?"

"Holy shit," Gabe mumbled.

Akihito rolled his eyes as he walked past, his expression indicating he'd heard it all before.

Joe grabbed Ethan's chin and planted a long, hard kiss on his lips.

"Let's make something clear right now," he muttered against the bartender's mouth as the latter melted into him. "The only thing getting penetrated in this relationship is your achingly sweet ass, and the only thing doing the penetrating is my rather splendid dick, capeesh?

Ethan hummed his acquiescence, his expression dazed, his fingers digging into Joe's shoulders.

"For the love of—*Will you two keep it in your pants?!*" Akihito hissed at the pair.

Gabe chuckled, his heart lightening for the first time that evening.

CHAPTER SIX

Cam swore as he studied the figures on the screen.

"*Damn it!* I thought we had everything sorted!"

One of the firm's junior managers hovered next to his desk, his expression pale.

"I'm sorry, Mr. Sorvino. We only spotted the error just now—"

Cam bit back another curse.

"It's okay, Keith." He glanced at the young man and the people lurking in the doorway behind him. "You did a good job, picking up on this. It would have been a disaster if we'd sent these files to the client." Cam took a deep breath and narrowed his eyes. "Here's what we're gonna do."

Cam raked a hand through his hair as his team scattered to do his bidding. He was angry with himself for having nearly made such a colossal rookie mistake.

It was his responsibility to do the final check on their client's investment files before submitting them. Although it had taken over a month to broker this deal and Cam had driven himself and his people to near collapse in the process, they had achieved the results they wanted and more. To have come so close to screwing it all up at the last minute was inexcusable, no matter how exhausted he may be.

Yet Cam knew it wasn't just fatigue that was messing with his usually unflappable intellect. A certain dark-haired man with ice-blue eyes had been at the forefront of his mind for the past three days, occupying his every waking moment and even his dreams.

The stupid argument he'd had with Gabe still weighed heavily on Cam's conscience. He knew he'd acted like a giant fool and should have picked up the phone and apologized by now. He'd even brought up Gabe's number several times but stopped at the very last moment, finger hovering above the call button on the touch screen.

What Cam needed to say and do would be best achieved in person, especially after the startling breakthrough he'd made in the last twenty-four hours of intense self-reflection. He'd poured all his energy into finalizing the business deal he'd been working on for over a month, anxious to return home and see Gabe, to tell him the decision he had finally come to. A decision that would impact both their lives and one Cam was eager to see through straightaway. It was the only way to shift this heavy weight from his shoulders, to get rid of the bitter taste that had been lingering in his mouth for far too long. To reclaim his lost future.

The sun was low on the horizon when he finally hit

the "send" button on the last email. Cam let out a ragged breath, pushed back from the desk, and glanced at his watch.

There were only three hours left before his flight. He'd anticipated he would have the entire afternoon to do what he'd initially planned.

Cam gritted his teeth.

There's no way I'm gonna let that stop me.

He mulled over his conundrum for a full minute before rising to his feet and walking out of his office. He frowned at Keith and the rest of his team where they sat at their desks in the open-plan space outside.

"I've got a question for you," Cam said gruffly.

Their eyes widened at his request.

GABE RUBBED A HAND ACROSS HIS EYES AND STARED blearily out of his office window.

It was past seven in the evening on a Friday. Night had long since fallen across Tokyo and car lights streamed on the busy streets outside, bright beams merging with neon signs. The riot of flashing colors mimicked the storm inside Gabe's heart.

Three days had passed since Gabe had hung up on Cam during their argument. Three days during which his lover had not rung or even texted him. Three days during which Gabe had barely slept.

Although they'd disagreed on things in the past, this was the first time they'd ever had a proper fight. Gabe was at a loss as to what he should do to bridge the growing distance between them. For all that he wanted to say sorry to Cam, Gabe also knew he deserved an apology for the selfish way the man he loved had acted that morning when he demanded Gabe not visit their friend's club.

"Go home," someone said harshly from the doorway.

Gabe startled. He twisted in his chair and eyed the brooding figure looming in the shadows outside his office.

"Hey, Wade," he muttered, his racing pulse settling. "I didn't know you were still here."

"Well, I am," Wade said gruffly, his blue eyes dark in the gloom. "I'm heading home, so it'd be great if you got your ass out of here too. I don't want word spreading that I'm a slave driver."

"But you are!" Gabe blurted out before he could stop himself. Heat flooded his cheeks in the next instant. He stared at his boss, chagrined at his sudden outburst.

A tired smile curved Wade's full lips. "You cheeky bastard."

Gabe relaxed. He looked past Wade's shoulder to the office at the far end of the floor.

"Has Rhys left?"

A strange emotion flashed across Wade's face before his expression grew shuttered. "Yes, he has."

Gabe blinked at his guarded tone. "Hey, are things —," he hesitated, "—are things okay with you guys?"

Wade stiffened.

"Why do you ask?" he said, his voice cool.

Gabe grimaced. "A blind man can see the tension between you lately."

Wade's smile turned bitter. He propped his shoulder against the door frame, just like Rhys had done several weeks before. "There's always been a lot of tension between Rhys and me. It's just never shown before now."

Unease filtered through Gabe as he studied Wade.

"Does this mean something is likely to happen to the company?" he said quietly.

Wade frowned.

"Why? Have the staff been talking?"

Gabe shook his head. "No. But we all hate seeing the two of you like this. And not just because Damon & Tucker is the kind of company anyone would kill to work for."

Wade's shoulders drooped for a moment.

"Don't worry about the company, Gabe," he said in a worn-out voice. "Damon & Tucker isn't going anywhere."

"I'm pleased to hear that," Gabe murmured after a pause. "You go on right ahead. I'll be out of here straight after."

Wade hesitated before nodding. He turned and disappeared in the direction of the elevators.

Gabe sorted through some documents before he shut down his computer and gathered his things. He'd just entered a lift when his cell rang. His pulse started a drumming beat as he stared at the caller ID. He tapped the screen and took the call.

"Hi," Cam said quietly from the other end of the line.

Gabe closed his eyes and leaned against the steel cabin, his knees going weak at the sound of Cam's voice.

"Hi," he said hoarsely.

Static suddenly jumped and echoed across the connection.

"Gabe—," Cam's voice came through brokenly as the lift rode to the ground floor, "I—we—"

"Cam?" Gabe stiffened and stared at the cell. "Cam, you're breaking up!"

He reached the lobby seconds later and jogged out of the building, checking the bars on his cell. The humid summer heat hit him like a wall, an oppressive mantle weighing him down instantly.

"Cam? You still there?" Gabe shouted in the mouthpiece as he rocked to a stop on the sidewalk, oblivious to the people slowing and staring at him.

"Going—tunnel—will—"

Gabe gritted his teeth in frustration as Cam's words reached him in fits and starts through a buzz of static. He headed briskly down the road.

"I still can't hear you, Cam. You're—" he started to say.

The static suddenly dissipated. Cam's voice came through loud and clear in the next moment, his words so stark Gabe thought his heart would stop.

"We need to talk."

Gabe's breath locked in his throat, his feet stilling on the ground. The rest of Cam's words washed over him as if from a distance, his gravelly voice saying things Gabe couldn't hear, didn't want to understand. The dial tone sounded as the call ended abruptly.

Gabe stared blindly into the night, the hand holding the cell falling limply at his side, the pain stabbing through his chest so sharp he knew this wound would never heal.

Oh God.

Bile twisted Gabe's stomach and rose in his throat. His worst fear was coming true.

Cam was going to break up with him.

Gabe swallowed the moan of agony building inside him and stumbled to the curb to hail a cab. There was only one place he wanted to be tonight. One place where he could lick his wounds and drown his sorrows. He couldn't go back to the apartment he shared with Cam. Not right now. Not like this.

Gabe gave the driver the address before leaning against the backseat and burrowing his face in his hands, the hot scald of tears prickling his eyes.

CHAPTER SEVEN

ETHAN STARED AT THE SOPHISTICATED BLOND SITTING AT the bar four feet to his left. His gaze moved to the dark-haired man lounging against the mahogany counter at the blond's side, a relaxed expression on his handsome face while they conversed in low voices.

It was rare to see Joe talk so easily to a stranger. Although Ethan knew the brooding club owner to be a wonderfully devoted and affectionate lover, it still irked Ethan that he had yet to uncover all of Joe's secrets.

Ethan finished mixing a couple of drinks, handed them over to the club patrons with a seasoned smile, and sidled up to the pair.

Joe looked at him with a quizzical smile when he stopped opposite them.

"Hey, Ethan." He glanced at the blond man next to him. "I don't think you've met Rhys before."

Ethan looked into a pair of curious baby-blue eyes while Joe made the introductions. He pressed his hands flat on the worktop behind the bar and leaned in closer to the two men.

"So, hey, I'm curious about something," Ethan said in a low voice, his gaze switching from the baby blues to Joe's hazel stare. "Did you guys used to be fuck buddies or something?"

Joe choked on his Scotch.

Rhys Damon blinked while the club owner went into a coughing fit. "Wow, so uncouth," he muttered. "What's it to you, kid?"

Ethan narrowed his eyes. He indicated Joe with a tilt of his head. "Well, that's my property right there, so I want to know if anybody's made any previous claims on him. And I kinda get this vibe when I look at the two of you."

Joe cleared his throat and gazed hotly at Ethan.

"Oh, so I'm your *property* now, am I?"

Ethan leaned in further and brought his face up to Joe's. "Why, yes. From your beautiful head all the way to your delicious toes." Ethan's gaze dropped to Joe's groin. "And I'm not even gonna mention that gorgeous co—"

Joe grabbed the back of Ethan's head with one hand and took his mouth in a searing kiss.

Ethan's pulse sped up at the electrifying feeling that wound through him and filled the space between them. It never ceased to amaze him how hot he could get for this man with a single touch, even though they had made love countless times before and knew every inch of each other's bodies.

"You minx," Joe whispered against his lips while a couple of customers clapped and cheered close by.

All the regular patrons at *Saron* knew of their relationship. Although some were chagrined at the fact that both Joe and Ethan were now officially off the market, most had been delighted at the unexpected development.

"Fuck me," Rhys said. "Are you two an item?"

Ethan dropped back on his heels, his ears warming at the promise he read deep in Joe's darkening eyes.

"We are," Joe replied gruffly, his heated gaze still on Ethan.

Ethan smiled slowly at his lover. "All shacked up and everything."

Though Joe still had the apartment above *Saron*, Ethan had sold his place in Bunkyo and they'd bought a new condo together in an exclusive area of Chiyoda, where they'd had their first date.

Ethan looked between Joe and Rhys again.

"So, you still haven't answered the fuck-buddy question."

Joe hesitated.

Rhys stirred his drink and directed a taunting grin at Ethan.

"A gentleman never tells."

Ethan frowned at the blond. "Somehow, that smile pisses me off big time."

Movement to the left distracted Ethan. He turned and saw a dark-haired figure heading for the bar, oblivious to the interested stares he drew from the men around him. Ethan stilled at the expression in the ice-blue eyes he knew so well.

Rhys turned and frowned at the newcomer.

"Gabe?"

Gabe looked blindly at the blond. He blinked, recognition dawning on his face as his sightless gaze focused for a moment.

"Rhys? What—what are you doing here?"

Rhys shrugged and indicated Joe. "I know this guy."

Gabe glanced dazedly between Joe and Rhys.

"What's wrong, Gabe?" Ethan asked sharply.

Gabe looked at him then. The pain reflected on his beautiful face made Ethan's stomach twist. He scowled.

What's that asshole gone and done now?

JOE CURSED AND SHIFTED GABE'S DEAD WEIGHT AGAINST his left hip. He patted the unconscious man's pockets, found the keys to Cam and Gabe's apartment, and let himself in.

Joe had never seen Gabe this drunk before. That the normally reserved man had downed four double Scotch in rapid succession within half an hour of walking into *Saron* had even shocked Ethan, who'd excused himself to the other two bartenders and dragged their friend upstairs to Joe's old place.

It was only after closing time that Joe got to the bottom of what was eating at Gabe.

"Cam's gonna break up with him," Ethan said bluntly when Joe entered the apartment.

Joe's alarmed gaze switched to where Gabe slept on the couch, his head on Ethan's shoulder, the dark shadows under his eyes telling Joe all he needed to know.

Joe frowned. "That's impossible. Cam is crazy about Gabe."

Ethan sighed, his expression stormy.

"That's what Gabe seems to think though. Cam phoned him tonight and said they needed to talk." He hesitated. "They had a fight a few days back."

Joe sat on the coffee table opposite Ethan and took his lover's hands in his own before studying the sleeping man beside him.

"What the hell happened between them?"

Ethan looked at him steadily, his green eyes darkening. "Gabe confessed."

Joe's pulse stuttered at the expression on Ethan's face.

Although they were now in a happy, committed partnership, it had taken over a year from the day they'd first met for them to get there. They'd both had to overcome Joe's stubbornness and his difficult past before they finally consummated their relationship. It hadn't helped that Ethan had been violently attacked by a stalker during that time.

Though Joe had imagined confessing his love to Ethan would be the hardest thing he would ever undertake in his life, it had been shockingly easy to do in the end. In fact, it had been as straightforward as breathing.

Joe wasn't sure Cam would find the process as

painless. His best friend had even darker demons to fight than he ever had and was ten times as stubborn. It was plain to Joe that Cam and Gabe were meant for each other. Gabe clearly knew this, too.

Joe squeezed Ethan's fingers. "I'll take him home," he said gruffly. He rose, hooked one arm under Gabe's shoulders, and lifted him off the couch.

"I'll call a cab," Ethan murmured.

The car arrived a few minutes later. Joe settled Gabe on the backseat and turned to Ethan where the latter stood in the private entrance leading to his old apartment.

"You going back home?"

Ethan hesitated. He shook his head, a faint smile on his lips.

"No, I'll wait here for you." He looked over his shoulder at the stairs leading up to the top floor. "It's been a while since we slept in this place."

Joe nodded and kissed him before climbing into the back of the cab.

The drive to Cam and Gabe's place in Ebisu took twenty minutes. By the time he got Gabe to their apartment, Joe's arm had started to ache from supporting the nearly unconscious man.

He sighed presently, hoisted Gabe over his shoulder, and flicked on a couple of lights as he headed down the corridor to the master bedroom. Gabe stirred when Joe lowered him to the bed. His lashes fluttered as Joe took off his shoes and socks.

Joe hesitated.

Might as well get him out of the jacket at least.

He leaned over Gabe and was peeling the suit off his shoulders when the latter blinked.

Gabe looked up at Joe fuzzily. His eyes darkened in the next moment.

"Cam," he breathed in a voice full of need.

He grabbed Joe's shirt, yanked him down, and kissed him.

Joe froze at the feel of Gabe's lips against his.

Gabe's grip loosened on Joe's shirt. He let go and fell back on the bed, out cold again.

Joe slowly straightened.

There was a noise at the door.

He turned his head and met Cam's shocked stare. Fury filled the gunmetal eyes he knew so well.

For Christ's sake.

CHAPTER EIGHT

"What the hell was—" Cam started in an incandescent tone, his heart pounding so violently at the sight he had just witnessed he thought it would leap out of his chest.

"You asshole," Joe said between gritted teeth. "Where the fuck have you been?"

Cam blinked rapidly, stunned for a moment. He scowled in the next instant.

"That's *my* fucking line!"

Joe raked a hand through his hair.

"No, it bloody well isn't." He sighed. "Let's clear up this misunderstanding right now. What you just saw was your boyfriend violating my lips, thinking I was you. Which, let me tell you, pisses me off to no end."

Cam stared, his pulse skittering in his veins. "What?"

"What's going on with you two?" Joe said gruffly.

Cam dropped his garment bag on his travel case, his

mind still reeling at what Joe had just told him. "What the hell do you mean?"

Joe put his hands on his hips and glared at Cam. "Gabe's been a miserable bastard the whole time you've been away, but even I was shocked at the state he was in tonight. He thinks you're breaking up with him."

Cam felt blood drain from his face.

"*What?*" Pain twisted through him as he stared blindly at the man on the bed. "He said that?!"

Relief flashed across Joe's face.

"So, you're not breaking up with him?"

"*No!*" Cam said vehemently. "If—if anything, it's the opposite—" He broke off, his eyes widening. "Oh, shit. The phone call."

Joe frowned.

"What phone call?"

Cam glanced at him dazedly.

"I was on the phone with Gabe when I was riding to the airport," he said hoarsely. "We got cut off just before my battery died. I told him we needed to talk."

Joe cursed. "Jesus, Cam. No wonder he was so upset."

Cam's shoulders sagged. He raised trembling hands to his head, his fingers twisting in his hair at the agony Gabe had no doubt lived through tonight.

"You mean, he's spent the last seven hours thinking—"

"Yes." Joe's expression grew sympathetic. "I don't know what's going on between you two, but I hate seeing you guys like this. You need to fix this, Cam."

Cam hesitated before dipping his chin.

"I—I know."

Joe studied him for a moment. "He loves you, Cam," he finally said. "Wholeheartedly. Irrevocably."

Cam shuddered and closed his eyes briefly, blood rushing in his ears at his best friend's blunt words.

"I know," he breathed.

Joe's cell rang. He slipped it out of his pocket, glanced at the caller ID, and took the call.

"Hi. Yeah, I'm still at the apartment. Cam just got here." Joe hesitated. "We were just talking things over." He looked at Cam. "They're gonna be fine. I'll make my way back now." Lines marred his brow. "Yeah, I know you're waiting for me." Joe's frown deepened. "What do you mean, you're sending me a picture?"

The phone dinged. Joe looked at the screen. His eyes flared.

"Is that my bow tie on his—" Joe brought the cell back sharply to his ear. "You little punk!" A slow smile curved his lips. "I'll be right there. Do *not* move an inch!"

Joe ended the call and crossed the floor to Cam.

"Ethan told me something once." He paused. "He said there was one way to make sure no one ever took him away from me. And that was to claim him as my own."

Joe looked over at Gabe and placed a hand on Cam's shoulder.

"Dare to be happy, Cam. Let go of your past and embrace the future before you."

Cam squeezed his best friend's fingers and

swallowed hard, his vision blurring. The sound of the front door closing reached his ears seconds later.

Silence descended on the apartment.

Cam let out a shaky breath and made his way to the armchair opposite the bed. He sagged into it and watched the sleeping man on the sheets for a long time, angry with himself for having been so stubborn and guilt-ridden by the unnecessary pain he'd inflicted on his lover.

And also just a little bit resentful about that kiss.

GABE STIRRED AND BLINKED FUZZILY. CURTAINS fluttered ahead of him. A hot breeze blew through the open window overlooking the terrace outside the bedroom and washed across his skin. He rolled onto his back, wondering why his head throbbed so much. Something tugged at his hands.

Gabe looked up and stiffened. A gray silk tie was wound tightly around his wrists, binding him to the sculptured bedpost in the middle of the leather and wood headboard.

Gabe's pulse jumped when he registered his near nakedness. He was dressed only in his briefs. A familiar smell reached him in the next instant, dousing his rising trepidation. He knew this scent.

Gabe scanned the shadowy bedroom, a different kind of nervousness suddenly skittering through him. His breath caught when he saw the man sitting in the chair opposite the foot of the bed, elbows on his knees, chin resting on the backs of his folded hands.

Gabe shivered, transfixed by the intense light in the gunmetal eyes studying him unblinkingly.

"Cam?" he whispered, confusion flooding his mind.

Cam rose slowly from the chair, his stance predatory as he approached the bed. He was still dressed in his work suit, the dark material clinging to his solid thighs and broad shoulders.

Gabe felt his cock twitch at the sight of Cam's commanding figure. He didn't know what was going on right now, why he'd been stripped and tied to the bed, or even how he'd ended up here in the first place.

The last thing Gabe recalled was sitting on the couch in Joe's old apartment above *Saron*, being comforted by Ethan.

Cam's gaze skimmed Gabe's body, his face inscrutable. Gabe bit his lower lip and squirmed under the laser stare. Despite the echoes of pain still coursing through his chest at the last words Cam had spoken to him, Gabe could not control his body's reaction to Cam's presence.

"About that conversation we had…" Cam said in a low voice, his eyes rising from Gabe's swelling arousal.

Gabe stilled when Cam met his stare head on. A fresh bout of agony twisted through him. He blinked back tears, his nails digging into his palms.

"I think you seriously misunderstood something," Cam continued, his gray gaze turning the color of a storm-swept sea.

Gabe's heart leapt and started a wild beat in his veins. He blinked, not sure if he'd heard Cam right.

"We're not breaking up." Cam reached up and slowly undid the knot in his red silk tie. "I'm sorry if I made you think that. I truly am."

Gabe inhaled shakily when he read the blazing truth in Cam's dark eyes.

Thank you, God!

Puzzlement replaced relief in the next instant. Gabe hesitated.

"Um, Cam, why am I—"

"Tied to the bed?" Cam cocked an eyebrow. "Oh, that's just the first part of your punishment."

Gabe's train of thought juddered to an abrupt halt.

"What?"

"For the kiss," Cam said, his voice hardening for a second.

Gabe stared, bewildered.

"What kiss?"

Cam narrowed his eyes.

"The one I saw when I walked in here tonight. You kissing Joe. In our bed, no less."

Gabe gasped. "*What?!* No way! I would never—"

Gabe stopped then, blood draining from his face. He thought he was dreaming earlier when he saw Cam hovering over him. He dimly recollected a pair of hard lips against his own. Gabe swallowed a groan.

Oh, shit.

"The guilty expression on your face tells me you remember what you did," Cam said coolly. He wrapped the ends of his tie around his hands and tugged slowly.

Gabe's mouth went dry, a shiver dancing down his spine as he focused on the taut red silk.

Fuck.

CHAPTER NINE

THEY HAD PLAYED WITH LIGHT BONDAGE DURING SEX before and Gabe had loved it. The feeling of powerlessness that swept over Gabe at those times was equally matched by his complete trust in Cam and the knowledge that he would only receive mind-numbing pleasure at the hands of his lover. And having Cam dominate him so thoroughly while he fucked him had given Gabe some of the most intense orgasms he'd ever had.

Cam's eyes flared, his widening pupils telling Gabe everything he needed to know about their current situation. His next words confirmed Gabe's suspicion about the dirty fantasy he hoped this was.

"I think I need to remind you who you belong to, Gabe."

Gabe stifled a whimper of excitement when Cam knelt on the bed and slowly peeled his briefs off his hips, his fingers raising tingles down Gabe's legs as they grazed his bare skin. Cam grabbed Gabe's knees next, pulling them up and tugging them apart, spreading his thighs open. The stormy gunmetal gaze swept Gabe from his head to his toes before pausing on the flushed head of Gabe's erect cock.

"So, here's what I'm gonna do." Cam lowered his head and dropped a kiss on Gabe's right knee. "I'm gonna use my mouth on you. And I'm not gonna stop until I'm ready. Even if you beg. Even if you scream. I'm gonna make you come over and over again before I take you. And, trust me, Gabe, when I take you, you're gonna be fucking ready for it."

Gabe's hips flexed reflexively at the filthy image Cam had painted for him in his husky voice.

Cam leaned over him and brought his lips to Gabe's left ear.

"One last thing," he whispered hotly, his breath sending shivers racing down Gabe's spine. "You're not gonna see any of this coming."

Gabe gasped when Cam gently placed the silk tie over his eyes and tied the ends around the back of his head, blindfolding him. Air shifted above him as Cam moved.

Silence descended on the room.

Gabe waited, his heart pounding so hard he wondered if Cam could hear it. He licked his lips nervously, ears straining for the slightest sound, the silk tie a red-stained darkness obliterating his vision.

Something soft landed on his face.

Gabe shivered when he recognized Cam's touch. He stilled, his entire body focusing on the fingers stroking his skin. His heart twisted at the achingly tender way

Cam explored his features, as if he were a blind man seeing him for the first time. Hope swelled inside Gabe's chest, choking his breath.

"Cam," he whispered shakily.

A hot mouth landed on his in the next moment, swallowing his gasp. Gabe moaned as Cam parted his lips and took over, urging his teeth apart, thrusting his tongue deep inside Gabe's mouth, the heated wet flesh wrapping masterfully around Gabe's own tongue.

Heat roared through Gabe at the torrid kiss. His cock twitched and his fingers bit into the silk tie binding him to the bed as Cam continued ravishing his mouth for a precious long moment, branding him, engraving his taste on Gabe's tongue.

Cam took his lips off Gabe's and moved to his left ear.

Gabe shuddered as he kissed, bit, and laved at the sensitive lobe.

Fingers skittered down his chest, featherlight yet scorching. Gabe moaned when Cam pinched and tugged at his hard nipples. Kisses landed on Gabe's neck, Cam's hair tickling the skin under Gabe's chin as he nudged Gabe's head back, exposing his throat for better access.

Pleasure stabbed through Gabe at the delicious assault. Cam knew all his weak spots and seemed intent on exploring them to their fullest tonight. Gabe swallowed a groan, not knowing whether to be elated or to cry at the sweet torture being inflicted on his aching body.

Gabe's pleasure grew exponentially when Cam

moved his clever lips and tongue from Gabe's throat to his chest.

"Cam!"

Gabe's cock throbbed as Cam took his left nipple in his mouth, his teeth grazing the sensitive, puckered flesh before tugging on it. He repeated the process with Gabe's right nipple and started alternating between the two, his hands skimming lightly over Gabe's chest.

Heat arrowed straight down to Gabe's dick as Cam continued tormenting his nipples. Gabe threw his head back on the pillow and rolled his hips, teeth biting into his lower lip, unable to control his body's thrusting motion.

Gabe moaned and gasped with every pull and suck of Cam's mouth. A familiar tension soon tightened his balls and coiled at the base of his spine.

"Oh God!"

Gabe shouted out Cam's name and stiffened, his back arching off the bed. His climax washed over him in violent shudders, his body convulsing and twisting on the sheets, his cock pumping hot cum onto his belly.

Gabe collapsed on the bed, heart hammering away against his ribs and shivers racing across his skin from his fierce orgasm. Fingers danced down his trembling thighs. They were followed by a torrid, wet tongue.

Gabe moaned as Cam touched and kissed his legs, finding the sensitive spots behind his knees and tormenting him until his cock throbbed and swelled again with fresh arousal.

There was a rustle next to his ears. Gabe felt a pillow slip under his ass, lifting his lower body off the mattress. His pulse stuttered when hard fingers curled around the backs of his knees, parting them wide before pushing them up, completely opening him.

Gabe shivered when a warm breath washed across the sensitive tip of his cock.

"*Oh!*"

Fire flashed through Gabe as his aching dick was swallowed inside a hot, wet mouth. Teeth teasingly grazed his shaft, running up and down his aching length for torturous seconds. Then, Cam wrapped his wicked tongue and lips around Gabe's cock and went to town on him.

"*Cam!*"

Gabe cried out, nails digging into his palms at the electrifying pulses of pleasure bolting through him. His hips rolled off the pillow as he thrust up and fucked Cam's eager mouth.

He came seconds later, his breath hitching in his throat as his entire body went rigid and his spine bowed off the mattress once more, his climax sending red light streaming across his consciousness while Cam continued sucking him.

Cam didn't stop when Gabe sagged back down on the bed, his busy lips and tongue working Gabe's dick until he was fully erect again, sending him over the edge once more.

Blood roared in Gabe's ears when Cam finally let him go, the shudders of his third orgasm still coursing through him. Gabe's ass twitched and his belly ached from the delicious tension, his mind foggy and his body limp with pleasure.

He felt the mattress dip and heard the slide of a drawer.

"Get on your knees, Gabe."

Gabe trembled at Cam's raspy command. He shifted up the bed, rolled, and closed his hands around the central bedpost. He rose up onto shaky knees and clung on for dear life.

The mattress dipped again behind him.

Hands closed on Gabe's butt cheeks and parted them, exposing the hidden cleft running from the bottom of his spine to the base of his balls. Gabe tugged his lower lip between his teeth, knowing what was coming next and dying to experience it.

CHAPTER TEN

"OH, FUCK!"

Gabe's mouth opened on a guttural moan at the first flick of Cam's tongue against the tight pucker of his hole. His hips flexed, his cock leaking pre-cum against his belly as Cam repeated the movement again and again.

Cam's fingers dug into Gabe's flesh, holding him in place while he kissed, licked, and sucked on Gabe's opening, making him melt from the intense pleasure of being rimmed.

Tension slowly wound through the base of Gabe's spine once more. His balls tightened, his orgasm building in delectable waves that had him bowing and arching like a cat. Cam continued rimming him with his wicked tongue, dipping the tip inside to tease and taste Gabe's hidden passage.

"Cam!"

Sweat rolled down Gabe's face as he climaxed savagely, cock twitching and pulsing out cum onto the bed, hips thrusting back against Cam's mouth and relentless hands, toes curling on the sheets.

Gabe felt Cam move and heard a faint click through the rush of blood pounding in his ears. Then, Cam was behind him again.

Gabe shivered when he felt cool wetness glide against his sensitive hole. Cam gripped his left hip and probed him with his lubed fingers. Gabe bit his lip and relaxed his lower body, opening himself up to his lover.

Cam glided two fingers in to the hilt and grazed his sweet spot, sending flashes of light across Gabe's inner vision and drawing a cry from his throat. Gabe's nails bit into the wooden post as Cam thrust repeatedly into him, his hips jerking with each bolt of pleasure.

"Oh! Oh God!"

Gabe shuddered as Cam slipped the thumb of his other hand inside him, stretching him further while he continued driving his slick fingers right up against Gabe's prostate.

Gabe's orgasm hit him like a freight train. He gasped as he came again, his shaft throbbing painfully as he spurted his release. A whimper escaped Gabe's lips when Cam continued fucking his pulsing, sensitive hole with his fingers.

"Cam! I—I can't!" Gabe begged. *"It's too much!"*

Hot lips pressed a searing kiss in the middle of his trembling spine.

"Not yet, Gabe," Cam said hoarsely.

Gabe's toes curled as he felt another climax wind through his lower body. He threw his head back and let out a harsh cry as he came once more, corded neck straining, fingers clutching the bedpost while the dizzying waves of pleasure stormed through him.

Gabe sagged a moment later, his knees finally giving way beneath him. He whimpered and twitched when Cam slipped his fingers from his spasming hole.

The mattress dipped. There was a clink of a belt buckle, followed by the slide of a zipper and the rustle of clothes. Gabe's ears flamed, his breaths coming in labored pants as he visualized Cam naked and aroused behind him. He swallowed a groan at the sound of foil ripping.

Gabe heard Cam's low grunt and knew he was slipping the condom over his cock. The mattress sank again as Cam climbed back on the bed.

Surprise flashed through Gabe in the next moment when Cam grabbed his waist and lifted him up into a sitting position. He gasped when he felt Cam set him down on his lap, Cam's strong thighs meeting the back of Gabe's, his heated cock coming to rub against Gabe's cleft, his chest kissing Gabe's sweat-slicked back. Gabe tugged at his lower lip with his teeth.

They'd never had sex in this position before.

Cam guided Gabe's hands back to the headboard and sucked Gabe's left earlobe. "Hang on," he whispered thickly.

Gabe dug his fingers into the wood as Cam hooked powerful arms under his knees and lifted him up. Air rushed out of him when he felt Cam's cock nudge his hole.

They both groaned as Cam slowly lowered him onto his shaft, impaling Gabe in one slick slide. A tortured moan left Gabe's throat at the mind-numbing sensation of Cam filling him to the hilt from this new angle and the feel of Cam's balls resting snugly under Gabe's own sac.

All coherent thoughts fled his mind in the next instant as Cam rolled his hips. Gabe cried out as light exploded behind his eyes, bright fireworks blooming and pulsing with each powerful thrust of Cam's cock into his hot passage.

Gabe bowed his head and lost himself in the moment, the potent pleasure intensified by his lack of sight, his entire being focused on Cam's electrifying touch and the erotic sounds their bodies made where they were connected, Cam's low grunts underscoring his own wild moans and cries.

Gabe's toes curled in empty air a moment later, his climax surging through him in long, agonizing waves. He chanted Cam's name over and over again as he came, his hole clamping down fiercely on the rock-hard shaft invading his passage, his own cock jetting out cum against his chest.

Cam sank his teeth into Gabe's shoulder. Gabe shuddered at the hot sting and heard Cam grunt and pant through his nose, his orgasm sending his cock swelling and rippling inside Gabe's body.

Gabe turned his head blindly, seeking Cam. He was rewarded with a blistering kiss that made him gasp and moan all over again, Cam swallowing the sounds as he swept his tongue inside Gabe's mouth, shivers coursing through both of them as their orgasms continued to pulse through them.

Cam dropped his face against Gabe's neck. His arms relaxed as he lowered Gabe's legs back on the bed, cock still wedged inside Gabe's twitching hole. Gabe leaned into him, his racing heart matching the violent pounding against his back, his labored breathing loud in his ears.

A moan left Gabe when Cam pulled out of his body. Gabe sagged on the bed and heard a rustle and the sound of another foil being ripped open. A hot kiss landed on the back of Gabe's neck. Heat flooded Gabe's cheeks in the next moment as Cam gently forced him onto his front. Cam slipped pillows under Gabe's belly before pushing him facedown onto the bed, the angle bringing Gabe's chest flush against the sheets while his ass rose in the air.

Cam spread Gabe's thighs and settled between his open legs. Slick fingers parted Gabe's butt cheeks a second later. Gabe groaned and closed his hands around the silk tie binding him, anticipation sending his cock twitching. The mattress dipped on either side of Gabe's head. Air shifted above him. Heat scorched Gabe's skin in the next instant as Cam positioned his chest flush against Gabe's back, crowding him deliciously on the bed.

Gabe let out a ragged breath when he felt the sheathed head of Cam's cock probe his opening. They both grunted as Cam slowly entered him. Cam nudged his shaft past the tight rings of muscle guarding Gabe's passage and slid home in one long, slick thrust.

Gabe gasped at the exquisite fullness of the

penetration. As with every time Cam took him, there was no sting, no burn. Only intense pleasure.

Cam pulled out and thrust inside again, his hips flexing slow and deep, his chest grazing Gabe's back as he started to fuck him sweetly.

Gabe lost himself to ecstasy as Cam took him from behind, the thrill of the submissive position making him bite his lip so hard he almost drew blood, his moans muffled by the sheets. His balls soon tightened against the pillow beneath his groin, his cock flexing and throbbing against the cotton.

The bed shook and squeaked as Cam accelerated his pace and started pounding Gabe's ass, the bite of his fingers on Gabe's hips and his heavy breaths heralding his impending climax.

Cam came savagely a moment later, his guttural grunts echoing around the room as he convulsed against Gabe, hips erratically pumping his pulsing cock in and out of Gabe's shivering hole. Gabe flexed his hips against Cam's groin and clenched his passage, prolonging the deliciously fierce penetration and Cam's climax, his own mind-numbing orgasm sending fire dancing through his entire body while he shivered and drenched the pillow with his hot cum.

Gabe shuddered when Cam suddenly pulled off his blindfold and undid the tie around his wrists. A groan left him with his next breath as Cam pulled out of his body. Cam rolled Gabe onto his back and tugged on his arms, lifting him up until he sat, facing him. He reached for the box on the nightstand.

Gabe blushed when he looked down at Cam's erect

shaft and the cum-filled condom still covering it. Cam discarded the used rubber, sheathed himself with a fresh one, and took Gabe's mouth in a torrid kiss, gray eyes stormy with desire and an undefined emotion.

Cam grabbed Gabe's butt before lifting him up against him. Gabe clung on to the strong shoulders below him and instinctively bent his knees. He wrapped his legs around Cam's waist, the angle bringing his throbbing opening flush against Cam's hot shaft.

Cam licked and nibbled Gabe's throat as he lowered him down onto his cock, the stiff head deliciously stretching Gabe's entrance again before he slid all the way inside. Gabe gasped and dropped his head back, his passage pulsing at the full penetration.

"You're mine, Gabe," Cam murmured hoarsely against his skin as he flexed his hips and started fucking him all over again. "Now and always."

Gabe moaned and sought Cam's lips, his fingers winding tightly in Cam's hair, his heart overflowing with emotion as he registered the stark truth blazing in Cam's gray eyes.

Then, he stopped thinking and surrendered to the passion and pleasure sweeping over him and Cam, their bodies moving in a thrilling sensuous dance, their breaths mingling as they kissed, their hearts beating wildly for each other.

CHAPTER ELEVEN

Light danced across the backs of Gabe's eyelids, faint but insistent. He sighed and buried his face in the pillow, his mind fuzzy and his body strangely sated.

The pillow moved under his cheek. Gabe blinked his eyes open. He stared groggily at the expanse of tan skin covering the hard chest rising and sinking beneath him. Awareness slammed into him in the next instant. Gabe looked up.

His heart skipped a beat when his eyes met a lazy gunmetal stare.

"Hi," Cam said softly where he lay, propped against the pillows.

Gabe swallowed.

"Hi."

He flushed when he recalled the events of last night.

Cam hadn't let go of him until dawn poked lightening fingers across the eastern skyline. They'd made love in their bed, against the walls, and quite literally all over their apartment, including the island in the kitchen, their very expensive couch, and the dining table. The last place they'd fucked was in the shower, after Cam went down on Gabe and gave him a screaming orgasm before savagely taking him against the tiled wall.

They'd changed the sheets and pillowcases before collapsing on the bed, sleep instantly claiming Gabe when Cam wrapped his arms around him and tucked his head against his chest.

Gabe shifted slightly on the bed presently. Despite the number of times Cam had taken him, his hole only ached pleasantly, Cam's skillful preparation ensuring Gabe's body was more than ready every time he sank his hard cock into Gabe's hungry passage. Heat flooded Gabe at the memory of how Cam had masterfully penetrated him time and time again throughout the night. His ass twitched again, his dick stirring against the sheets.

Cam sighed.

"So, I've been a gigantic moron."

Gabe blinked, his arousal dimming as he studied Cam's repentant expression. His heart twisted when the agony of yesterday's emotions washed over him once more.

Cam's eyes darkened at what he read on Gabe's face. He touched Gabe's lips gently.

"I never meant to hurt you, Gabe."

A lump formed in Gabe's throat. He nodded shakily at Cam's heartfelt apology and turned his head to kiss Cam's palm, peace filling him as he inhaled his lover's scent.

Cam took a ragged breath.

"I've been thinking a lot over the last few days. About what you said back at the inn."

Gabe stiffened.

"Cam, you don't have to—"

The rest of Gabe's words were swallowed by Cam's lips as the latter leaned down and kissed him fiercely. Gabe moaned breathily at the possessive way Cam claimed his mouth.

Cam let go a moment later and pressed his lips against Gabe's forehead. "Don't," he whispered. "Don't apologize for your feelings for me. I couldn't bear it if you did."

Gabe's heart lurched at Cam's words. He looked up, searching Cam's face wildly for the truth he could read in his voice. Hope flared inside him at the light blazing in Cam's gray eyes. Gabe's breath caught in his throat all over again. He swallowed convulsively.

Cam smiled tremulously and brought Gabe's left hand up to his lips. He dropped a scorching kiss on Gabe's skin, his gaze still locked on Gabe's eyes.

Gabe's heart stuttered in his chest when he finally registered the beautifully elegant white gold and platinum band adorning his own ring finger. How he hadn't registered the weight of it until then was a shocking mystery to him.

Confusion dawned inside Gabe as he stared at the gleaming metal Cam had slipped on his hand while he slept. It was erased by the sudden, insane conviction that jolted through him with his next heartbeat, robbing him of air once more.

"Cam," Gabe whispered, not wanting to pin all his hopes on what the ring meant.

Cam rose and knelt on the mattress. He pulled Gabe up until he sat on the bed opposite him before cradling Gabe's face in his hands. He gently pressed their foreheads together.

"I've been a fool," Cam said huskily, staring into Gabe's eyes. "I thought I would be fine so long as I closed off my heart to anyone who tried to get too close. I never wanted to fall—" He swallowed hard, his fingers trembling on Gabe's skin. "I never wanted to fall in love. I didn't want that burden, didn't want to make myself that vulnerable again to another person, didn't want to take the risk that someone else would tear my soul apart and leave me broken once more, like she did all those years ago."

Gabe's breath hitched in his throat, his vision blurring while his chest swelled with emotion. The lack of bitterness in Cam's voice as he spoke of his mother told Gabe everything he needed to know about his lover's heartfelt confession.

Cam kissed him then, his lips featherlight as they danced across Gabe's mouth.

"I never knew what I was missing out on until the night you walked into my life." Cam smiled and rubbed his nose against Gabe's. "I think I fell for you then. When our eyes met for the very first time. I was just too much of a stubborn ass to realize it."

CHAPTER TWELVE

Tears welled up in Gabe's eyes and spilled down his cheeks.

Cam inhaled shakily before gently stroking his fingers across Gabe's face, wiping away the wet trails before kissing his flushed skin.

"I'm sorry I made you wait so long for this," Cam murmured. He closed his eyes briefly, his pulse racing at the powerful emotions swirling through his chest and clogging his throat.

Gabe's breath caught again when Cam opened his eyes and looked at him steadily.

"Gabe Anderson, I love you with all my heart," Cam said, his gaze locked on Gabe's glistening cobalt-blue stare. "Will you be mine, now and forever more?"

Gabe shuddered when Cam reached across to the nightstand and picked the second wedding band. He placed it in Gabe's hand and kissed his palm before stilling and watching him.

Gabe stared at the ring for a silent moment before looking up at Cam.

Cam's breath locked in his throat at the emotion shining brightly on Gabe's face. He cursed himself once more for having been a fool for so long.

He never knew it could be so easy to love someone. Never knew the words could leave his lips so effortlessly, as if he were drawing a simple breath. Never knew it would be so painless to chain himself to another person, to entrust his heart and soul to someone else's care.

"Yes." Gabe nodded tremulously, a dazzling smile curving his lips. "*Yes!* A thousand times, yes! I—"

Cam groaned and took Gabe's lips in a passionate kiss that sent a hot tingle to his dick. He let go of Gabe reluctantly and held his left hand up. Gabe swallowed and slipped the gold and platinum band on Cam's finger.

They linked their hands and stared at the perfect, matching, gleaming rings.

"How—when—," Gabe finally stammered, glancing up at Cam.

Cam smiled.

"I thought I would have had most of yesterday to choose our wedding bands. Turned out, I ended up with only three hours before my flight."

Cam chuckled as he told Gabe how his entire team had pulled out all the stops to secure him an urgent appointment with the best jeweler in Singapore. That the man had had the exact rings Cam had been looking for when he went to the exclusive shop had seemed like fate.

"And the rest is history," Cam said. He grimaced. "Well, apart from my stupid cell dying and you thinking I was bailing out on us—"

Gabe grabbed Cam's face and kissed him fiercely.

"Don't," he breathed against Cam's lips. "I'm sorry I overreacted. I should have trusted you."

"And I'm sorry I was such a dick about you going to *Saron*," Cam murmured.

Gabe smiled. "You were. A giant dick."

Cam grinned and arched an eyebrow.

"I didn't hear you complain about the size of my cock last night."

Gabe flushed and looked down. Cam's dick twitched and stirred at Gabe's heated stare. He stifled a groan when Gabe reached out and touched him.

"I love your cock," Gabe breathed. He curled his fingers around Cam's thickening shaft and dipped his head to kiss the broad head.

Cam hissed, fire darting through him.

Gabe settled down on his belly and started licking and sucking Cam's cock. His eyes closed as he worked Cam's hardening length with his fingers, lips, and tongue. A moan hummed past his lips and vibrated against Cam's sensitive flesh, causing him to curse.

Cam grabbed the lube from the nightstand and warmed a dollop of the cool liquid between his hands. He reached down Gabe's back and delved into the shadowy cleft at the base of his spine while the latter continued skillfully blowing him.

Gabe gasped and arched against the mattress. He parted his legs, giving Cam access to his hole.

Cam groaned when he dipped lower and reached Gabe's tight pucker. It twitched at his touch. Another moan ripped from Gabe's throat and sent a jolt of pure pleasure pulsing through Cam. Cam played with Gabe's folds and the tight stretch of skin leading to his balls, his fingers repeatedly circling and teasing the rim of Gabe's opening, causing it to clench and spasm.

Gabe's hole unfurled a moment later. Cam dipped two fingers inside and grunted when Gabe tightened his passage around him, sucking him deeper. Gabe's mouth mimicked the motion of his lower body, his strong jaw working Cam's cock further inside his throat.

"Fuck, Gabe."

Cam shivered as delicious tension spiraled through his body.

He worked Gabe's hole for another minute before slipping his fingers out. He moved Gabe's eager head off his throbbing cock and rolled him onto his back.

Gabe let out a soft moan and parted his thighs with his hands. Cam's heart clenched at the sexy picture his man made where he lay on their bed, body opening up as he surrendered himself for Cam's possession.

Cam reached for a condom and was about to rip the foil with his teeth when Gabe closed a hand around his wrist.

"No," Gabe breathed. He glanced at Cam's straining erection and flushed slightly before meeting Cam's eyes. "I want—," he swallowed, "—I want you inside. Bare."

Cam groaned and took Gabe's mouth in a blistering kiss, his heart pounding at the sexy, filthy wish the man he loved had just expressed.

Cam knew Gabe was clean. Cam had gone to his own doctor and had himself tested when they started going out. He had never taken someone bareback before. Never known what it felt like to enter a man raw, to feel his hot passage cradling his naked cock.

"Are you sure?" Cam murmured against Gabe's mouth, excitement sending his pulse racing even faster.

Gabe looked up at him and nodded shyly. He reached down and trailed his fingers along Cam's shaft before clasping his dick, causing him to swallow a curse.

"I want to feel you, Cam," Gabe said huskily. "All of you. Deep inside me."

He tugged at his lower lip with his teeth, the move so sensual that Cam could not help the way his cock twitched and throbbed in Gabe's fingers.

Gabe let go of Cam's dick and wrapped his arms around Cam's shoulders. He lifted his head off the pillow and brought his lips to Cam's left ear.

"I want you to come inside me, Cam. I want you to take me and fill me with your seed."

The last of Cam's restraint snapped at Gabe's sexy, taunting words. He worked lube feverishly onto his naked dick before settling between Gabe's thighs. Gabe lifted his legs and wrapped them around Cam's mid back, his eyes hot with need.

Cam propped his elbows on either side of Gabe's head and lowered his body flush against Gabe's. They both groaned and arched into one another as Cam's naked cock gently stroked Gabe's hole.

Cam rotated his hips and teased Gabe for tantalizing seconds, causing him to gasp and moan. He swallowed a groan, the thrilling sensation of his bare cock against Gabe's wet opening sending bolts of electricity jolting through him.

"Cam! *Please!*" Gabe cried out.

He dug his fingers into Cam's back and dropped a heel to Cam's left butt cheek, urging him closer.

Cam finally gave in to the man begging him so sweetly. He leaned down, took Gabe's mouth in a soul-scorching kiss, and nudged his hips forward.

CHAPTER THIRTEEN

"*YES!*" GABE SHOUTED.

Gabe's eyes widened at the feel of Cam's naked cock parting his opening. He gazed dazedly into Cam's heated gunmetal stare while the blunt head of Cam's dick stretched the rings of muscles guarding his passage. The sensation was unlike anything Gabe had ever experienced, so filthily exquisite he thought he would come there and then.

"*Cam!*" Gabe gasped as Cam continued gliding inside.

Cam let out a grunt when Gabe tightened reflexively around him, his passage squeezing Cam's naked shaft and sucking him in deeper. Sweat beaded Cam's forehead and upper lip as he flexed his hips and slid fully home. He stilled above Gabe, his body rigid with tension.

They stared at each other for timeless seconds, reveling in the achingly sweet rite heralding their first true mating.

"Cam," Gabe breathed, his heart thundering against his ribs. "Does it feel—"

"*So fucking good, Gabe!*" Cam hissed. He closed his eyes and nudged his hips forward, causing Gabe to gasp again. "It feels *so* good inside you!"

Gabe moaned as Cam pulled out before thrusting back in, the pleasure rippling through his body from the raw friction so intense he doubted he would last long.

Cam grunted above him and set a sweetly punishing pace, his hips flexing and rolling slowly, torturing Gabe's sensitive passage with each withdrawal and deep glide of his thick, hard cock.

Gabe clutched Cam's shoulders and curled his toes into Cam's back as a delicious shiver raced down his spine. His balls tightened under his aching dick.

Gabe came seconds later, his hoarse cry of pleasure echoing across the room while he pulsed out hot cum against their bellies.

CAM GRITTED HIS TEETH AND LOOKED TO WHERE GABE'S dick throbbed between their bodies, jetting out thick streams of creamy fluid, Gabe's musky scent filling the space between them.

He cursed as Gabe's hole pulsed with his orgasm, the rhythmic contractions sending bolts of ecstasy shooting through Cam's aching, hard cock. Riding Gabe bareback was the most incredible thing Cam had ever experienced. He couldn't believe how hot and tight Gabe's passage felt around him, how much more he could sense each of Gabe's moans and gasps as they vibrated through his body, as well as every intimate pulsation of his opening.

Cam hooked his left arm under Gabe's right thigh and lifted his leg up, dropping Gabe's calf onto his shoulder while he continued pumping steadily in and out of Gabe's body.

Gabe moaned and met Cam's gaze with a glazed expression, color staining his cheekbones a glorious pink as he found himself opened even wider for Cam's possession.

Cam looked down and stilled when he saw the place where their bodies connected.

Fuck.

Cam flexed his hips slowly and watched his naked cock glide out of Gabe's wet hole, the taut rim dragging along the sensitive surface of his shaft. He pushed forward and groaned when his dick slowly disappeared inside Gabe's body, heat and tightness gripping him once more.

"*Cam!*" Gabe gasped.

Cam glanced at him.

Gabe bit his lower lip, his face flushed. His expression told Cam he was hungry for more.

Cam looked down to where their bodies connected once more and accelerated his pace. He cursed at the intense feel, sight, and sounds of their raw mating.

"*Cam! Oh God, yes!*" Gabe cried out. He chanted Cam's name over and over, head twisting and thrashing on the pillow as pleasure coursed through him, his hard cock rubbing against Cam's belly. He came again a moment later, his spine arching off the bed, his orgasm so powerful he nearly lifted Cam up as he helplessly thrust his hips upward.

Cam gritted his teeth as the familiar sweet tension wound through his thighs and gathered at the base of his spine. His balls tightened and rose in his sac. He bowed his back and finally gave in to his instincts, gripping Gabe's thigh tightly while he thrust powerfully in and out of his body.

Gabe shuddered and moaned, his passage pulsing strongly, the fading ripples of his orgasm doubling back as he neared another climax, his glazed eyes meeting Cam's heated stare.

Sweat pooled from Cam's face and dripped onto Gabe's chest as he fucked him deeply and thoroughly, the bed rocking and creaking with each powerful propulsion of his hips, the erotic soundtrack inflaming his senses further.

Cam's orgasm swirled through him in slow, delectable waves, ebbing and flowing with each sweet pull of Gabe's tight passage, swelling teasingly until it grew past the point of no return.

Cam stilled and arched his spine as his climax washed over him, his breaths leaving his throat in harsh grunts, the pleasure so intense it was almost pain. He pinned Gabe's hips to the bed and pumped violently into him, filling his insides with his cum.

Gabe cried out and raked Cam's back with his nails as his own orgasm finally struck, his body convulsing violently beneath Cam, corded neck tensing as he bowed his head back.

Cam leaned down and bit Gabe's exposed throat, a savage feeling of possession sweeping over him as he continued thrusting and pulsing deep inside the man he had claimed as his own, drowning his hungry passage with his seed. Cam didn't stop until Gabe's hole finally relaxed and he collapsed on the bed, his entire body shivering with pleasure, his labored breathing and soft moans sweet music to Cam's ears.

Cam moved Gabe's legs back down on the bed, twined their hands together on the pillow on either side of Gabe's head, and lowered his trembling frame onto Gabe's, his face finding the crook of his lover's neck.

They lay like that for a long time, their sweat-slicked skin kissing intimately, their thundering hearts vibrating against the other, their bodies still connected.

A shudder ran through Gabe a moment later.

"Wow," he breathed.

Cam looked up and kissed the dark locks plastered to Gabe's forehead. "You okay?"

Gabe blinked dazedly.

"I don't think I can move."

Cam chuckled.

They both groaned when the action shifted Cam's cock inside Gabe's body. Cam grunted and carefully slipped out.

"Oh." Gabe bit his lip and blushed.

Cam looked between Gabe's thighs. His cock twitched when he saw his sticky cum pooling out of

Gabe's twitching hole. Filled with wonder, he reached down and stroked a thumb across the flushed folds.

Gabe moaned and squirmed beneath him.

Cam stared from the wet, warm pad of his finger to Gabe's glowing face. His pulse sped up at the raw, possessive feeling that swept over him once more as he gazed into Gabe's dazzling eyes.

Cam wanted it again. Wanted to take Gabe, to claim him, to own him, to mark him, to flood his insides with his seed once more.

"Let's clean you up," Cam said fervently. He dropped a hot kiss on Gabe's lips, rose to his knees, and pulled him up to a sitting position.

Gabe stared when Cam climbed off the bed. His ears grew bright red as he studied Cam's swelling arousal.

"Um, that's fine, but why do you look like you're raring to go again?"

Cam shrugged. "What can I say? You have that effect on me."

Gabe sighed.

"Seriously though, I really don't think I can move."

Cam grinned. He hooked his arms under Gabe's shoulders and knees and ignored his lover's shocked gasp as he lifted him off the bed.

"For better, for worse, right?" Cam said thickly.

Gabe inhaled sharply at the fragment of the wedding vow, his ice-blue eyes turning cobalt as Cam turned and headed for the ensuite bathroom. He wrapped his arms around Cam's neck and kissed him.

CHAPTER FOURTEEN

"I NEED SOME DICK ACTION."

Gabe choked on his Scotch. Cam thumped his back as he coughed and spluttered.

"For fuck's sake, Eveline," Cam said, glaring at the beautiful blonde sitting on the barstool next to them.

Eveline Claude—AKA Madame Claude, their friend and the owner of *Le Secret*, the high-end escort service Joe Cavendish used to work for—gazed morosely into her cocktail. She downed the drink and slammed the glass on the mahogany counter, oblivious to the stares she was getting from the men around her.

She was the only woman in *Saron,* bar Michelle the singer.

"I mean it. My vajayjay is gonna dry up at this rate."

"Oh God," Ethan muttered. He dropped his forehead against a shelf full of bottles where he worked behind the bar and thumped it repeatedly for several seconds. "Kill me. Kill me now."

Gabe smiled. He knew Ethan and Eveline got on

like a house on fire and were as close as a brother and sister could be—which was a miracle, considering how long Ethan had harbored a misguided grudge against her concerning her relationship with Joe.

Eveline slid her body forward across the counter, her arms dangling limply over the worktop behind the bar. She eyed the man on the other side of her.

"Hey, Rhys, fancy a fuck?"

Rhys Damon cocked an elegant eyebrow and stirred his drink.

"No, thanks. My dick won't get hard for you."

Eveline sighed. "You're right. I don't think I could get wet for you either."

Ethan groaned. "Jesus, Evie."

Joe appeared beside the bartender. He paused when he saw Eveline, his hands stilling on a bottle of water. "What the hell is wrong with her?"

"She's in heat," Cam muttered.

Gabe swallowed a chuckle.

Joe stared at Eveline. "I thought things were going well with the sheikh."

Eveline sniffed.

"The sheikh is an ass. I mean, literally. That guy loves having his hole played with. I'm all for strapping on a dildo and fucking someone, but the dude's gay. He just refuses to admit it."

"Some guys are just dicks like that," Rhys muttered, lines marring his brow as he stared into his glass.

"I know, right?" Eveline murmured. Her expression brightened as she studied Rhys. "So, what's up with you these days?"

Rhys narrowed his eyes at her. "You just want to hear the sordid details of my sex life, don't you?"

Eveline grinned unashamedly. "The dirtier, the better."

"Well, I'm sorry to disappoint you," Rhys drawled with a wry smile. "I'm afraid I've been having a bit of a dry spell, too."

Gabe stirred at the bitter light that flashed in Rhys's eyes. He didn't know much about Rhys's personal life apart from the fact that he and Wade Tucker seemed to be on the warpath right now. Although the two friends and partners were at odds most days, they hadn't let the strain in their relationship affect their business, for which Gabe and his coworkers were grateful.

Eveline stared at Rhys.

"*What?*"

She straightened on the barstool and waved her hand vaguely at Rhys, from his blond head all the way down to his polished shoes.

"How? I mean, look at you. If I were a gay man, I would want a piece of your real estate."

Rhys chuckled. "Thanks. I think."

Gabe startled, not quite sure he'd heard Eveline right.

"You're gay?" he asked Rhys in a stunned voice.

Gabe flushed at the battery of stares that came his way. It finally sank in why Rhys had been hanging around *Saron* so much these days. Gabe had assumed it was simply because he was friends with Joe.

"Wow, your gaydar is so bad," Ethan muttered.

"His gaydar is broken," Eveline stated flatly.

"He ain't got no gaydar," Akihito muttered as he strolled past them.

Rhys's eyes twinkled as he observed Gabe. He slid off his barstool, walked around Eveline, and wedged himself between Gabe and Cam.

"So," Rhys drawled, tilting Gabe's chin with the tip of one finger, "now that you know the truth, fancy a tumble between the sheets, Mr. Anderson?" He smiled sexily and leaned toward Gabe. "I'm a natural bottom, but I can top, too," he murmured in Gabe's ear.

Heat flooded Gabe's cheeks. He swallowed at Rhys's teasing expression.

"No one is topping anybody," Cam said silkily. He took Rhys's hand and gently lowered it from Gabe's face.

Rhys raised an eyebrow and glanced at the metal band on Cam's ring finger.

"Oh, we're Mr. Possessive now, are we?"

Cam smiled fiercely. "You'd better believe it. Gabe is mine."

Gabe's pulse skittered at the jealousy blazing in the gunmetal gaze he knew so well. Although ten days had passed since that fateful weekend when Cam confessed and proposed to him, Gabe was still walking on clouds, his chest filled to bursting with love. Their friends' obvious delight after their initial stunned reactions at seeing the wedding bands on their hands had warmed Gabe's heart further.

Gabe could hardly believe how deliriously happy he was and how thoroughly the man beside him fulfilled him. He had never felt so whole, so complete, so alive.

He knew Cam thought the same from the number of times they had had sex since that day.

Gabe's ears warmed as he recalled their passionate lovemaking the night before. Cam had filled Gabe's insides with hot cum four times before he finally relented and pulled out of Gabe's pleasantly aching hole.

"Besides," Cam added, "I've had enough of seeing other men paw my property."

Gabe twitched, a sliver of guilt stabbing through his chest.

Eveline perked up.

"Huh?" She glanced between Gabe's flushed face and Cam's slightly grim expression. "Who's been manhandling this sweetie?"

Gabe glanced at Joe.

Eveline's eyes widened.

"*Noooo!*" She covered her mouth with her hands and stared at Joe.

Joe slowly capped the bottle of water, sighed, and turned to the silent, green-eyed blond beside him. "Look, Ethan—"

"I'm sorry," Gabe blurted, remorse filling him at Ethan's expressionless face. "It was my fault. I was drunk. I didn't know what I was doing."

Joe raked a hand through his hair. "He thought I was Cam. It was only a kiss—"

Ethan moved. He walked over to Cam, grabbed his tie, yanked him down across the counter, and kissed him hard.

The noise level in the club dropped. Michelle the singer stumbled over her words onstage.

Gabe opened and closed his mouth soundlessly as the wet smooching noise echoed along the counter, vacillating between shock and intense jealousy.

Ethan abruptly let go of Cam and narrowed his eyes at Joe.

"I think we're even now."

"For fuck's sake," Cam muttered, wiping his mouth with the back of his hand.

The horror painted across Cam's face caused Gabe's anger to dissipate instantly. He swallowed the laughter suddenly threatening to erupt.

Joe glared at Ethan.

"Oh, yeah?"

Joe stormed toward Rhys, curled one hand around the back of the blond's head, and pulled him in for a kiss.

Michelle dropped the mic. Gabe gaped. The noise level in the club rose to an uproar.

Joe released Rhys and eyed Ethan smugly.

"*Now*, we're even."

Rhys blinked, his blue eyes slightly glazed where he half-leaned across the counter. "Shit. I think I just got hard."

Ethan scowled at Joe before twisting on his heels.

Gabe blinked when his friend's stormy green gaze landed on him.

"Um, wait a minute—" Gabe mumbled.

It was as far as he got before Ethan grabbed his

shoulders and planted a wet one on his lips. Cam swore.

Akihito stopped beside them and sighed.

"I know everyone's pretty busy playing tonsil tennis right now, but I have something important to tell you. Madame Claude's panties just self-combusted."

Ethan lifted his mouth off Gabe's. They all turned and stared at Eveline's flushed face and parted lips.

"Wow, I think I can see smoke coming out of her vajayjay," Rhys muttered.

Eveline grunted and stared between Joe and Cam.

"What?" Joe said.

"It's your turn," Eveline said hoarsely.

Joe and Cam glanced at each other.

"No fucking way," Cam said.

"I love him like my brother but, no," Joe stated flatly.

Eveline squirmed on the barstool.

"You assholes. I deserve a peep show after what you just put me through."

Ethan let go of Gabe's shoulders and sighed.

"Are you out of your sweet mind?"

"Come on." Eveline stared from Joe to Ethan and Cam to Gabe. "You won't even notice I'm here."

"No," Cam said stonily. He wrapped a possessive arm around Gabe's shoulders and tugged him into his chest.

"Nuh-uh," Joe muttered. He crossed over to Ethan, folded his arms around him from the back, and dropped his stubbled chin on Ethan's blond locks. "No one gets to watch me and sweet cheeks here do the hot and dirty."

Ethan flushed and gripped Joe's arms where they were wrapped around his waist, his eyes gleaming with contentment.

Eveline chewed her lower lip, her expression turning thoughtful.

"How about if I leave a camera in the room?"

"The camera would explode," Joe stated, deadpan.

Cam sniffed. "Yup."

Gabe blushed.

"You fuckers." Eveline grinned slowly, her blue eyes twinkling with genuine delight. "I swear, you four look so happy, you kinda make me wanna gag a little."

"I'm right there with you, sister," Rhys muttered. He handed Eveline a glass of Scotch and toasted her. "Flaunting their blissful relationships in front of single people."

"And their hot bodies," Eveline said with a nod before taking a sip from her glass.

"And their big cocks," Rhys added.

"Not to mention, their huge wallets."

Rhys paused. "Is that a euphemism for giant dicks?"

"No. I really mean, huge wallets." Eveline indicated Ethan. "Wonder boy over there is a fucking genius when it comes to the stock market. And his IQ is off the charts."

Cam grunted. "She's right. The brat's gifted."

Rhys blinked slowly at Ethan.

"Wow. He looks like he barely graduated high school."

Ethan narrowed his eyes at Rhys. "That's it! Next

time this asshole comes in here, I'm gonna slip him a laxative."

Gabe chuckled. Cam's chest started shaking behind him. Joe grinned. Eveline giggled. Rhys muttered something rude under his breath, his lips curving in a smile.

The club patrons stared at them as they dissolved in laughter.

THE END

What happens when a brooding, billionaire guardian clashes with the sexy ward he can never touch?

Get Sweet Obsession (Nights #4)
Turn the page to read an extract now!

SWEET OBSESSION (NIGHTS SERIES BOOK 4) SPECIAL PREVIEW

CHAPTER ONE

THIS ASSHOLE!

Ash Colby scowled at his watch. He took a shallow breath, uncrossed his legs, and propped his elbows on his knees. The motion brought pain surging across his temples. The migraine had been with him for the last two hours. Although he would have loved to blame it on the humidity of Singapore's late September monsoon season, Ash knew his current circumstances had led to the headache jackhammering against his skull. The fact that he'd just gotten off a seventeen-hour flight from San Francisco wasn't helping either.

Ash rubbed a hand across the back of his neck before glaring at the secretary seated behind the modern walnut desk to his left.

"He knows I'm waiting, right?" Ash snapped.

John Peace sighed and nudged his smart, black-rimmed specs up his nose.

"Yes, Ash. Luke is aware that you've been waiting a while."

"Forty fucking minutes is not a while, John," Ash said between gritted teeth.

"Language, Ash," the secretary murmured.

Ash looked around the chic marble and wood waiting room overlooking a panoramic vista of the dazzling city and sun-kissed bay beyond the glass wall behind the secretary's desk.

"There's no one else here."

John ignored Ash's acerbic observation and studied him steadily.

"You look a bit peaky. Would you like some water?"

Ash scowled. He knew the secretary was only trying to be helpful, but he was past caring at this point.

"No, I don't want fucking water, John. I want to know why my lord and master has summoned me all the way here from Stanford five days before term starts."

Ash couldn't help grind his teeth as he recalled the terse phone conversation from two days ago. The motion exacerbated the band of tension gripping his head and raised his ire further.

"Luke would like to see you," John had said coolly when he'd called Ash at eight on a Sunday morning.

Ash frowned as he walked through the front door of his condo. He dropped his gym bag on a chair and headed to his bedroom.

"What's this about, John?" he said, irritated. He sat on the edge of the bed, kicked off his shoes, and fell backward onto the sheets. "And when did he get back to San Francisco?"

John hesitated. "He isn't in San Francisco."

Ash blinked at the ceiling before slowly sitting up, his incredulity quickly turning to anger.

"Wait a minute. You're telling me Luke is in Singapore and he wants me to go there to see him? Fuck no!" he growled.

John sighed. "This is important, Ash. You know Luke wouldn't make such a request unless it was an urgent matter."

Ash rubbed a hand across his eyes and swallowed hard. There was no denying the truth in the secretary's words.

Luke Rutherford, Ash's former guardian and the current custodian of his rather substantial trust fund, was not a fickle man.

Ash inhaled shakily and tried to quell his rising temper. "Can you at least tell me what this is—"

Someone took the phone from John.

Ash froze when Luke came on the line.

"A car is coming to pick you up in thirty minutes. Pack a bag and be ready. The jet's already at the airport."

Ash stared blindly ahead as the line suddenly went dead. He listened to the dial tone for a stunned moment before flinging the phone across the room and throwing himself back on the bed. A cry of rage left Ash's lips as he raked his hands through his hair. Despite the fury and frustration burning in his veins at Luke's outrageous command, Ash could not help the shudder of awareness that raced through him after hearing Luke's voice.

It had been over a year since they last spoke.

For one insane moment, Ash considered not obeying the man who quite literally owned him, body and soul. The man he had been in love with for as long as he could remember.

The man who had broken his heart and shattered his dreams five years ago, on the night of Ash's seventeenth birthday.

The thought of the possible reprisals Luke would visit upon him if he did not get on that plane sent a quiver of apprehension through Ash. The guy was capable of anything. Just as Luke had promised, the car arrived promptly at eight thirty and Ash lifted off from San Francisco International Airport an hour later.

Ash sighed, his thoughts returning to his current predicament as he leaned back on the expensive Barcelona chair and propped his feet on the coffee table. He ignored John's disapproving stare and indicated the walnut door opposite from where he sat with a jerk of his head.

"So, who does he have in there? Must be someone damn important if he's ignoring me for this long." Ash paused. "Not that the asshole doesn't ignore me on a regular basis anyway."

John pinched the bridge of his nose. "I would really appreciate it if you didn't keep calling Luke an asshole, Ash. And, yes, he's got his asset manager in with him right now. Mr. Sorvino flew in from Tokyo yesterday and is heading straight to Japan after their meeting."

"Yippee for Mr. Sorvino," Ash muttered. "Lucky bastard. I hope I'm back on the jet tonight as well."

John hesitated. He opened his mouth and closed it soundlessly.

A tendril of unease shot through Ash as he stared at the secretary's face. He narrowed his eyes. "What?"

"Nothing," John murmured.

Ash was still studying him suspiciously when Luke's door opened. A man walked out of the office.

The stranger was tall and dark, with a commanding presence that had as much to do with his handsome face and his arresting gunmetal eyes as it did with his incredibly ripped body. Had Ash not been unreservedly in love with Luke, he would have found the guy captivating.

A figure appeared behind the asset manager. Ash's mouth went dry when Luke stepped out of the room.

At six foot two, Luke Rutherford's hard bodied, toned frame more than matched the man beside him. With dark hair that most women would kill to sink their hands into, finely trimmed stubble that framed a strong, angular jaw, and amber eyes that had the power to silence a crowded room, Luke Rutherford was not only sinfully attractive, he was also the embodiment of a successful businessman and billionaire.

Ash swallowed.

Sexy fucker.

Read Sweet Obsession today

AFTERWORD

To all my friends who helped make this possible. You know who you are.

To you, my readers. Thank you for reading Gabe and Cam's second story. Their happy ever after is coming soon! I would be grateful if you could leave a review on Goodreads or on the store where you purchased this book if you enjoyed it. Reviews help readers like you find my books and I truly appreciate your honest opinions about my stories.

Make sure to sign up to my store newsletter for special deals on my books and new release alerts. Or you can sign up to my author newsletter instead to get upcoming release notifications, sneak peeks, and giveaways.

ABOUT THE AUTHOR

Ava Marie Salinger is the romance pen name of an Amazon bestselling author with a passion for writing addictive tales. Known for her action-packed and thrilling urban fantasy novels, she has expanded her repertoire with the introduction of the M/M urban fantasy romance series Fallen Messengers. Additionally, she has penned the scorching hot contemporary M/M romance series Nights and Twilight Falls as A.M. Salinger. When not immersed in her writing, Ava can be found curating inspiring music playlists, indulging in her love for nature, marveling at the latest gadgets, and savoring Chinese cuisine.

You can find all of Ava's books on her author store at
shop.adstarrling.com